Let's Get Wheeling

Originated by Polly Dunbar

WALKER BOOKS
AND SUBSIDIARIES
LONDON · BOSTON · SYDNEY · AUCKLAND

Everyone wanted to go riding.
Tilly found her old tricycle, but it was too small.

"You must have grown, Tilly,"
said Pru.

It was a perfect fit for Hector.

He rang the bell and
pedalled off.

Doodle found a skateboard.

Beep beep.
Pru whizzed by in her car.

"Pru coming through!"

Tumpty found a nice red bicycle.

It looked just the right size for Tilly.

"I don't know,"
she said.
"It's quite big."

Doodle hit a bump and went flying.

Luckily she landed safely on a cushion!

Tumpty found roller skating a little scary.

SQUEAK!
SQUEAK!

But with Tilly's help he soon got the hang of it.

Whizzz

Tiptoe found a scooter and was off.

Soon everyone was riding happily
around the garden.

Everyone except Tilly.
"I'm worried I might fall off,"
she said.

"We'll help you!" said Hector.

"You can do it!"
said Tumpty.

Everyone helped Tilly learn to ride the new big bike.

"You'll be OK, Tilly!"
said Doodle.

Soon Tilly was riding on her own.

"Brilliant, Tilly!" called Tumpty.

"This is fun!" called Tilly.

Now everyone
had wheels.
Round and round
they rode.

What a wonderful wheelie day!

BEEP!
BEEP!

First published 2013 by Walker Books Ltd, 87 Vauxhall Walk, London SE11 5HJ

2 4 6 8 10 9 7 5 3 1

© 2012 JAM Media and Walker Productions
Based on the animated series TILLY AND FRIENDS, developed and produced by Walker Productions and JAM Media
from the Walker Books 'Tilly and Friends' by Polly Dunbar. Licensed by Walker Productions Ltd.

This book has been typeset in Gill Sans and Boopee.

Printed in China

British Library Cataloguing in Publication Data:
a catalogue record for this book is available from the British Library

ISBN 978-1-4063-4831-6

www.walker.co.uk

See you again soon!